The Story Girl
Book 8

Dedicated to my six grandchildren, the "cousins," especially to Bethany, for whom I began this journey with the "Story Girl" on "The Golden Road," six years ago. I pray all of you will find these stories about the King cousins a wonderful example for you to follow in holiness, purity, and real fun—and help you along your own journey to the heart of God.

From the author of Anne of Green Gables

L.M. Montgomery

The Story Girl
Book 8

THE WINDS OF CHANGE

Adapted by Barbara Davoll

zonder**kidz**

www.zonderkidz.com

SEP 2 9 2005

The Winds of Change
Copyright © 2005 The Zondervan Corporation, David Macdonald, trustee
and Ruth Macdonald

Requests for information should be addressed to:
Grand Rapids, Michigan 49530

Library of Congress Cataloging-in-Publication Data

Davoll, Barbara.
  The winds of change / by Barbara Davoll ; adapted from The story girl
by L.M. Montgomery.
    p. cm.–(The story girl ; bk. 8)
  Summary: As summer turns to fall on Prince Edward Island, the King
cousins participate in a wedding, enjoy a family reunion, and prepare to
bid each other farewell.
  ISBN 10: 0–310–70862–1 (softcover); ISBN: 978–0310–70862–9
  [1. Storytellers — Fiction. 2. Cousins — Fiction. 3. Conduct of life — Fiction.
4. Prince Edward Island — History — 19th century — Fiction.
5. Canada — History — 19th century — Fiction.] I. Montgomery, L. M. (Lucy
Maud), 1874-1942. Story girl. II. Title.
  PZ7.D3216Wi 2006
  [Fic]–dc22   2004012269

Editor: Amy DeVries
Interior design: Susan Ambs
Art direction: Merit Alderink
Cover illustrations: Jim Griffin

Printed in the United States of America

05 06 07 /OPM/ 10 9 8 7 6 5 4 3 2 1

Contents

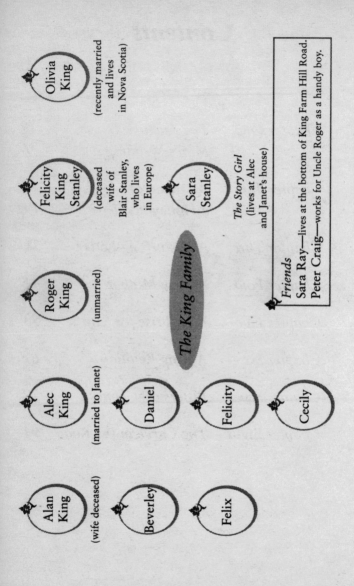

The King Family

Alan King (wife deceased)
- Beverley
- Felix

Alec King (married to Janet)
- Daniel
- Felicity
- Cecily

Roger King (unmarried)

Felicity King Stanley (deceased wife of Blair Stanley, who lives in Europe)
- Sara Stanley — *The Story Girl* (lives at Alec and Janet's house)

Olivia King (recently married and lives in Nova Scotia)

Friends
Sara Ray—lives at the bottom of King Farm Hill Road.
Peter Craig—works for Uncle Roger as a handy boy.

The Awkward Man's Wedding

Just then we heard a loud shriek and a crash of glass. We looked up just in time to see Felicity, punch bowl and all, in a heap on the floor. Peter Craig, who had a tremendous crush on the beautiful Felicity, was trying to pick her up off the floor.

Chapter One

The Story Girl and I both got up early the morning Jasper Dale and Alice Reade were to be married. I was wakened by a warm sun slanting across the room where my brother, Felix, and I slept in the old King farmhouse. I dressed hurriedly and nearly ran right into Sara Stanley on the stairway.

"Why are you up so early?" I asked Sara.

"Too excited about the wedding to sleep, I guess," was her reply. "I'm so glad you're up early, Bev," she continued. "I could really use somebody tall to help with the decorating at the church. Could you possibly bring the ladder up from the barn and help take it over to the church in the pony cart? Maybe you could stick around and help us get the trellis up on the platform too."

I looked at Sara Stanley with disgust. "I was planning to go fishing with the fellas this morning, Sara. Can't you girls handle the decorating? I know we fellas said we'd set up the chairs for the reception, and I don't mind helping you get the ladder over to the church," I added. "But I figured you girls would handle all the rest of the frills and fripperies."

"Oh," she said in surprise. "I thought *all* of us cousins were going to help Miss Reade. Felicity is totally tied up making the sandwiches and cookies for the reception. She and Cecily have been up since dawn working on them. So the decorating is all mine. I need to be finished decorating at the church by noon so I can get dressed with the bridesmaids. Felicity is already over at the Golden Milestone getting the punch bowl and table ready."

Golden Milestone was the name Jasper Dale gave his beautiful old farm home. That was where the wedding reception would be after the ceremony at the church. As I listened I saw Sara did make sense. The girls couldn't do all that needed to be done by themselves. Feeling sheepish, I reluctantly agreed to help Sara at the church and to get the other fellas started on the chairs. This wedding was important to our girl cousins. Miss Reade was their piano teacher, and our whole community was excited about the marriage of "Beautiful Alice" and Jasper Dale, the "Awkward Man."

Oh, I forgot to introduce myself to you new readers. My name is Beverley King, but my *friends* call me Bev, especially if they want to *stay* my friends. I'm not sure why my mother chose that name, which is kind of "girlish," but I think as you get to know me you'll see there's nothing girlish about me. I have to admit it has been a challenge being a boy and having to put up with my feminine name.

The Story Girl, Sara Stanley, and I are the oldest of the six King cousins. Well, actually there are eight of us who hang around together—eight counting Peter Craig and Sara Ray. Peter is Uncle Roger's handy boy and lives with him in the house next door. Sara Ray, as I mentioned, is Cecily's best friend and lives down at the foot of the King Farm Hill Road. Sara Ray is a big crybaby, but we put up with her for Cecily's sake. It's really a pain having two girls in our group who have the same name. That's one of the reasons we call Sara Stanley the Story Girl.

My brother, Felix, and I are from Toronto. We have been staying with our Uncle Alec and Aunt Janet while our father is in South America on business. We were only supposed to stay for a year, but Father allowed us to stay longer.

"I hope you don't mind helping me," Sara Stanley said doubtfully, looking at me with those big brown eyes of hers. Who could say no to such eyes?

"Naw, I guess not," I agreed, trying to show an enthusiasm I really didn't feel.

Maybe I ought to tell you a little about our wedding couple. The groom's name is Jasper Dale.

Before you laugh at his name, let me tell you that he has a nickname too. He's called the "Awkward Man." I don't think names are all that important. I mean, having to live with the name *Beverley* all my life has helped me feel a bit of sympathy for people with strange names.

I've heard that he was given his nickname when he was a young man and just starting to attend parties. At one event, he spilled punch all over a girl. In trying to clean up the punch mess, he fell over his feet and dumped the whole punch bowl over himself and her. The other kids hooted and laughed at him so much that he was too embarrassed to ever go to another party. They began calling him "awkward" and the name stuck, even after he was grown. He was a quiet and shy man anyway, so he mostly stayed at home except for church.

But when beautiful Alice Reade came to town, something wonderful happened. She and Jasper got acquainted—she didn't think he was awkward at all. Before half the silly sisters in Carlisle knew it, Jasper and Alice were engaged. Their romance was swooned over by the sillies that had made lots of fun of Jasper before. And now their wedding day will be the event of the year. You can imagine how the tongues are wagging in our little town. A lot of the fellows have bets on whether Jasper can get down the aisle without tripping. The girls are all gossiping about what "dear Miss Reade" will do if he does trip, and whether their children will be like her or him. Good night! I say let them get married first!

As Sara and I were going out the door to get the pony cart, Princess Felicity came into the kitchen. She isn't really a princess, but she thinks she is. She had already been to Golden Milestone and needed more silver dishes from our farm for the reception. To be fair to Felicity, she is an incredible cook and a hard worker. If anyone can put together a fine wedding reception, she can. It's just her bossy attitude that is so hard to take.

"Where do you two think you are going so early?" she asked in her snooty tone that implied we had no right to do anything she hadn't approved.

"Bev's going to help me with the decorating for the wedding," Sara answered in a fairly civil tone. Sometimes it's awfully hard to keep your tones civil around Felicity.

"I can't imagine how much help he'll be since he doesn't know a flower from a weed," Felicity retorted nastily. "But of course Miss Reade wouldn't ask me to help with any of the dirty work. She said she thought I'd be pretty as a rose serving at the punch bowl."

"Yeah, one with thorns," I jabbed as we left the kitchen.

"I'm sorry, Sara," I apologized, as I loaded the ladder in the pony cart and we started down the lane. "Felicity brings out the worst in me."

"I understand, Bev. You and a lot of others, I'm afraid," said Sara soothingly.

There was a buggy at the church when we arrived. Pastor and Mrs. Marwood were already there decorating.

"Glad to see you brought some help, Sara," called the pastor as we entered the church.

Mrs. Marwood was tying lace bows on each pew. "We need to get the candle globes from the parsonage and also the aisle runner," she said. "Both are in a box on our front porch."

"Come on, Bev, let's go get them in your pony cart," the pastor said.

When we returned, Mrs. Marwood and Sara had everything in place so that the flowers could be added quickly. In an hour all of the decorating was finished. The old church had never looked lovelier. As we were getting ready to leave, another buggy drove into the churchyard.

"Oh, it's Jasper!" cried Mrs. Marwood. "I forgot he was bringing the trellis."

The pastor and I rushed outside to help Jasper bring in the trellis. He had done a beautiful job making it. Sara and Mrs. Marwood decorated it quickly with white flowers and greens. "There!"

said Mrs. Marwood, dusting herself off when they had finished. "That was just the finishing touch that was needed, Jasper."

As we walked out of the church, Jasper pulled his watch out of his pocket and checked the time. "We have little more than an hour before the wedding. I need to hurry," he said with a smile. Bowing graciously to the ladies, he folded his long legs into his buggy and drove off with a rattle.

Sara and I climbed into the pony cart and headed home at a fast clip. It was a short way, but it gave us some time to talk about the remarkable change we saw in Jasper Dale.

"Jasper really did look handsome, didn't he?" Sara remarked.

"He did," I agreed.

"Why do you suppose Miss Reade could see past all the negative stuff people said and fall in love with him?" Sara asked.

"Because she took the time to think about it," I answered. "And she's not so centered on herself as *some* people we know."

Sara knew I was talking about our cousin Felicity. Felicity was beautiful, but she never had a thought for anyone but herself.

"I'm sure Felicity will look gorgeous today at the wedding," Sara said.

"Just like a rose," I said, quoting Felicity's remark earlier in the day.

"And *I'm* going to look like a *thorn* if I don't hurry," Sara said, jumping out of the pony cart and rushing into the house.

The next time Sara and I had a chance to talk we were at the reception at Jasper Dale's beautiful home.

Mrs. Griggs, Jasper's housekeeper, had everything under control, and the young ladies from the village were keeping the buffet line flowing nicely. It seemed like the whole county was there. No one had been inside Jasper's home since his mother died, and all were pleasantly surprised to see how elegant and beautiful it still was.

Sara and I stood just inside the dining room door, balancing our plates of goodies and cups of punch.

"You know I'm not as silly as some girls are about all this," she said, "but I thought I would melt when Jasper looked at her for so long before he kissed her."

"What surprised me was when Alice tripped on her long veil and Jasper caught her in his arms," I remarked. "It was as though he'd been catching women in his arms all of his life."

"No one will call him the 'Awkward Man' now," Sara prophesied. Just then we heard a loud shriek and a crash of glass. We looked up just in time to see Felicity, punch bowl and all, in a heap on the floor. Peter Craig, who has a tremendous crush on the beautiful Felicity, was trying to pick her up off the floor.

"What happened?" I asked my brother, Felix, who was holding his sides laughing at the sight of snooty Felicity in such a mess.

"Sh—she was trying to refill the punch bowl," he gasped, with tears coming down his face from laughter. "She got the pitcher caught on that big bow on her dress and fell into the punch bowl, face down. The punch bowl fell to the floor and—"

"And no one got hurt," said Jasper Dale quietly, coming up behind us. "Mrs. Griggs will have this cleaned up in no time. We have another bowl of punch ready, don't we, my dear?" he asked, addressing his bride.

"Certainly," said the bride in her quiet way as she headed off to take care of things. Sara and I found our way out to the porch where we could pull ourselves together from laughing. "It looks as though our 'pretty little rose' got drenched," Sara giggled.

"Well, roses do need watering," I responded.

Just then Sara elbowed me in the ribs. "Bev, look!" Just around the corner of the porch, we saw old Billy Robinson paying off Cyrus Brisk. It seems

Billy thought he had a sure thing when he bet Cyrus that Jasper Dale would trip going down the aisle. Instead, Jasper had caught his lovely bride in his arms when *she* tripped. Sorry, Billy. You can't be a winner all the time.

A Dream of a Honeymoon

"Felix King," said Felicity with her
hands on her hips, "you know we made
a solemn promise to always tell each
other our dreams. Now you must tell us
what you dreamed—just as you promised!"

Chapter Two

The next morning the wedding was the main topic of conversation at the breakfast table.

"Oh, didn't Miss Rea—uh—Mrs. Dale look lovely," gushed Felicity. "That antique satin dress was so beautiful and elegant." She gave a little spin to show off as she placed the flapjacks on the table.

"She did look nice," agreed my pudgy brother, Felix. He said this without even looking away from the flapjack he was loading up with lots of butter and maple syrup. "I hope someday I can find a bride as beautiful as Mrs. Dale," he remarked.

"You'll never find anyone to have you if you keep on eating the way you do," laughed Felicity. "No woman wants a fat bridegroom. They'd have to *roll* you down the aisle."

"It's all right, Felix," soothed our sweet cousin, Cecily. "You are very comfortable to be with, and that counts for a lot." Cece could always find a way to make a person feel at ease when under Felicity's fire.

"I thought the trellis Jasper made was great," said Dan. "That was not easy to design. He's some regular guy."

"That's not what I heard you saying about him last week when you were placing bets about him making it down the aisle without tripping," needled Felicity.

"Well, at least I didn't spoil the reception by falling into the punch bowl, my graceful sister," he swiped back.

"Let's not get into this," said the Story Girl wisely. "I am so excited to hear they are able to go to Europe for their honeymoon. Imagine! Staying in a castle in Scotland."

"I didn't know the Dales had Scottish relatives. Have you ever heard about that before, Sara?" questioned Cecily.

"Well, yes. Mrs. Griggs mentioned it one day while I was helping her with her canning. I saw the old coat of arms over the fireplace in the kitchen and asked about it. She mentioned that Jasper's father came from someplace in Scotland, and they were related to Scottish royalty."

"What else did she say?" questioned Felicity. "I would *think* you would have told us something important like that."

"I guess I didn't think it was all that important," answered Sara quietly.

"Well, I should say it is," said Felicity. "I think it is quite important to know who your neighbors are. Especially if they are *royalty!*"

Dan rolled his eyes at me. None of us liked the way Felicity always treated someone that was important a lot nicer than ordinary folks. I thought of the time the governor's wife came to tea and Felicity got put in her place.

It was fun to remember how she had mistakenly used tooth powder instead of sugar for the cinnamon toast. It was even more fun when the governor's wife found out.

"What's the smirk for, Bev?" Dan grinned.

"N–nothing," I stammered, embarrassed at being caught.

"Maybe you were thinking that Princess Felicity will be practicing up on her Scottish shortbread recipes so she can properly welcome the 'royals' home from their honeymoon. She won't want to make a mistake like she did when the governor's wife came to tea," Dan said.

"Oh, stop it, you two," Felicity said, jumping up and beginning to clear the table. "I just wanted to hear a romantic story if there is one."

"Well, there isn't exactly a story, but Mrs. Griggs did tell me some interesting things," admitted the Story Girl.

"Tell us, Sara," urged Cecily.

"Tell us what?" asked Peter Craig, coming in the kitchen door without knocking. This summer was to be Peter's last working for Uncle Roger. His father had recently returned and become a Christian. Now that his father had stopped drinking and was taking care of the family, Peter wouldn't have to work. He could go to school like other boys. We were all going to miss him since he wouldn't go to our school, but we were happy for him.

"Sara was just going to tell us how Jasper Dale is related to Scottish royalty. You know they are staying in a castle in Scotland on their honeymoon," Cecily informed him, with her soft brown eyes wide with interest.

"Ya don't say!" said Peter, forking the flapjack that Felicity was offering him. We all knew that Peter and Felicity liked each other. Peter always defended her behavior when she was nasty to us. How could he help but like her? She was so beautiful. This morning her cheeks were prettily flushed from cooking, and the little white-frilled apron made her look like a doll. Too bad she had a cantankerous spirit that could turn milk sour.

"Do tell us, Sara," urged Felicity, sitting down after clearing the table.

"Well, Mrs. Griggs, Jasper's housekeeper, said she heard the story from old Mrs. Dale, Jasper's grandmother. It seems that Grandmother Dale was a beauty in her day. She was born the only child of a Scottish couple, who were the head of a large clan up in the Highlands of Scotland. They lived in a beautiful castle and were very wealthy.

"A young American man, who was taking a tour of Scotland, met the beautiful Scottish girl and fell in love with her. Her mother and father opposed the marriage, so the young couple ran away and took a boat to America. Once here, the young Scottish woman bitterly missed her home in Scotland.

"Since the young man was himself wealthy and could live anyplace he wanted, he brought her here to Prince Edward Island. They soon met other Scottish folks and she felt better.

"They became farmers here on our Island and eventually built the beautiful old home they call Golden Milestone. The relatives in Scotland have kept the castle in good repair, passing it down to the present owners. All the Scots had hoped that someday there would be a reunion of their family. And now there will be. Jasper and Alice will become the new owners of the castle," said the Story Girl, finishing the story.

"Oh, you don't suppose they will stay over there, do you?" asked Cecily with tears in her eyes. "I'm sure dear Miss Rea—uh—Mrs. Dale deserves to live in a castle, but we would miss her so."

"I don't think they will stay," replied Sara. "Jasper told me he was looking forward to visiting Scotland, but he said he wouldn't be comfortable there for long. I think he loves his home here on the Island and so does Alice."

"Oh, it is just like a dream," sighed Cecily, her eyes twinkling with unshed tears. "To think how the Awkward Man has become almost like a prince. Imagine how they will love being in Scotland and having their honeymoon in a castle."

"I wonder how long they will stay in Scotland?" said Felix.

"Jasper told me that he has his harvest workers all lined up, so I'm sure he will be back in time to oversee all that," I answered.

"Speaking of harvest, I guess I'd better get back to the field. I wouldn't want your Uncle Roger to fire me for not being on the job," said Peter.

"I'll walk out with you," said Felicity. "It's your turn to wash the dishes, Sara. Cecily will help you," she said in her bossy tone.

Dan rolled his eyes at me again. Felicity was starting to sound just like our Aunt Janet. Our aunt depended on the girls a lot during the summer when she had to work out in the garden early in the morning. The guys and I headed for the fields to help Uncle Alec. The sun was beginning to feel hot already.

The next morning at breakfast, Felix came to the table late, looking like he had lost his last friend. His clothes were rumpled, and his hair, which was usually perfect, was uncombed. He stumbled into his chair and tucked something under him. Normally Aunt Janet wouldn't let us eat if we came late to breakfast. But sometimes she looked the other way if it were Felix. I think she was a bit easier on him since he was the youngest boy and didn't have a mother.

She put the scrambled eggs in front of him and said, "You look like something the cat dragged in, Felix. Aren't you feeling well?" She looked at him carefully.

Uncle Roger, who was eating breakfast with us that morning so he could help Uncle Alec with the haying, glanced at Felix with an amused twinkle in his eyes.

"What have you got tucked under you, Felix?" he asked. Uncle Roger was the biggest tease in the province and sometimes very annoying when he decided to make fun of us. I could see my brother was not doing well, and I felt a protective sense of outrage that Uncle Roger should tease him.

Felix's ears turned red instantly, as they always did when he's embarrassed. "Uh—it's—my Dream Book," he said, almost in a whisper.

"Your Dream Book?" repeated Aunt Janet, whirling around from the stove to get a better look

27

at Felix. "I thought we told you children not to fool with those anymore. I specifically told you, Felix King, that there would be no more eating before bed so you could have bad dreams."

She was referring to a contest we were having to see who could have the worst dreams. We had discovered that by eating terrible concoctions before bed, our poor digestions caused us to have magnificent dreams. All of us recorded those dreams in a Dream Book.

"Felix King," said Felicity with her hands on her hips, "you know we made a solemn promise to always tell each other our dreams. Now you must tell us what you dreamed—just as you promised!" Felicity glared at Felix, as we all did.

"You won't like it," he said under his breath to Felicity.

"*I* won't like it! What does it have to do with *me*?" the exasperating girl demanded.

"What *does* it have to do with Felicity?" repeated Uncle Roger, hoping to hear a good gossip tidbit.

"Please don't make me tell you," my miserable brother begged Felicity.

"I *insist* on knowing," said our snooty cousin.

"Well, all right," said Felix. "I've figured it out— why I dreamed it, I mean. Do you remember, Felicity, when you said I was so fat they'd have to roll me down the aisle when I get married?" He looked at her with the question.

Felicity began to squirm and look uncomfortable. We all looked at each other across the table with big eyes. *What was coming next,* we wondered. The old clock on the mantel gave a bong on the half hour. Felix swallowed and sighed loudly.

"Well, I dreamed I was at my wedding all dressed up and ready to go down the aisle. The—best man made me sit down and gave me a push with his foot to roll me down the aisle. As I rolled down the aisle it became a long hill outside. I rolled and rolled and ended up at the bottom of the hill. My bride was there waiting for me. She was a big, black, fat cat with your face, Felicity, and your hair. There was something else too. Beside the cat that looked like you, was Peg Bowen's black boiling pot waiting for me."

Oh my, if you could have seen Felicity's face! She turned white as a sheet and jumped up from the table. Uncle Roger was laughing so hard that he had pushed his chair back against the wall, blocking Felicity from getting away from the table.

I thought Dan was going to explode. Between gasps of laughter he said, "How appropriate, my sweet sister. A feline Felicity! Meow! Meow!"

Aunt Janet was furious. Taking hold of Felicity's arm, she said quietly, "Did you truly say that awful thing to Felix?"

Felicity had to admit she did. "Go to your room this minute, my girl," she said. "You will learn, Felicity, or I will die trying to teach you, that words can hurt more than sticks and stones. Your long tongue will trip you up every time you use it to hurt another. Apologize to Felix and then to your other cousins who have witnessed your rudeness."

Felicity did so and left crying bitterly. This was one of many times that Aunt Janet had to step in and save Felicity from herself. Felix's "dream of a honeymoon" was truly a nightmare. Several years later, I read his Dream Book with his permission. That dream was not recorded, and he did *not* win the dream contest.

A Disturbing Letter

*"It's a lot to think about, isn't it, Felix?"
Uncle Alec said with understanding. By this
time, tears were coming down Felix's chubby
little face, and they were stinging my eyelids
too. A big change was coming into our lives.*

Chapter Three

The days were speeding by. Somehow we knew that once the summer ended things would change for us King cousins. That made each day feel like a gift. One afternoon all of us hid away in one of our favorite places—the loft of the old barn. We were all there, even Cecily's good friend Sara Ray, and Peter Craig, who had been given some time off while Uncle Roger went to town. We were all sitting around munching on the raspberry tarts Felicity had made for us.

Sara Stanley sat in the open window of the hayloft dangling her bare feet, humming a little tune, while her cat, Old Paddy, leaned against her, licking the last delicious bit of raspberry from her fingers. It was Sara who broke the contented silence.

"These tarts are simply delicious, Felicity. You should enter them in a contest."

"Oh, they aren't as flaky as they usually are," she simpered in a voice filled with fake humility. "I'll keep practicing."

"Don't you just hate for summer to end?" inquired Cecily, who was trying to put on Paddy a grass chain she had just made.

Just then the garden gate clicked, and Aunt Janet came through it. She looked up at us from down on the ground. "Yoo-hoo," she called, waving her hand. "Felix and Beverley have a letter from their father. Come and get it, boys."

We scrambled to our feet and clattered down the loft steps. A letter from Father, although short and just the bare facts, usually arrived right on schedule each Friday. What was unusual was that we had not heard from him for a month. To tell you the truth, I had been feeling a little worried about him. South America is a long way from Prince Edward Island, and in those days there were horrible diseases that could take lives quickly.

"Oh, I hope he's all right," said Felix. I could tell he was also relieved to hear something.

I breathed a sigh of relief as I saw the familiar writing on the envelope. If he were sick, he probably wouldn't be writing the letter himself.

"Do hurry, Bev," urged Felix. "I hope he tells us why he's not written yet this month."

Father's greeting was always the same. "My Dear Sons," he began. I smiled at Felix, trying to reassure him that everything was normal. The letter was two pages long this time, which was unusual for him. I led the way over to a log where we could sit down and read comfortably. This is what the letter said:

My Dear Sons,

I hope you will forgive me for not writing each week this month. I do thank you for your letters to me though, and hope when you hear my reason for not writing, you will understand. No, I have not been sick. In fact, I am better than you can imagine. Our new business here in South America is working out very well. I am now the South American director. That promotion has given me fine opportunities to promote and build the line here in Brazil. That is part of the reason I have been so busy.

However, there is something else that has been keeping me occupied. Last year I met a lovely woman through one of my business contacts. Her father is lieutenant governor of the province of Quebec. She is a widow, a few years younger than I, and has one delightful little daughter, whose name is Caroline. Isn't it interesting that she and I would have to come to Brazil to meet each other?

Her name is Elizabeth Creighton, and to make it short, my dear boys, I have fallen in love with her. Imagine this, she has some

distant relatives who are related to us. Anyway, I never dreamed that such a thing could happen to me — to us, that is, because you both are my highest concerns. Boys, do you think you could find room in your lives for a new mother and sister? If you have any doubts, please let me know.

By the time you receive this letter, Elizabeth, Caroline, and I will be in Toronto so that I can meet her family. I, of course, want you to meet them as well before we make further plans, so the three of us will be arriving in Carlisle next week for a visit. I am writing Alec and Janet the particulars of our arrival. I plan to stay with your Uncle Roger next door, and hope Janet can find room for Elizabeth and Caroline. I know this is sudden, but I feel certain when you meet them both, you will love them as I do.

One more thing. I know it is never easy for children to embrace a new mother. May I assure you that no one can ever replace your dear mother in my heart or yours. Sweet Caroline, who is six years old, is very dear and looking forward to having two big brothers. Until next week, I send my dearest love.

Father

"He sounds like it's a done deal," said Felix with a very sober face.

"Well, maybe not," I answered. "I'm sure he'll wait to make his final decision until we have had a chance to meet them."

"Don't kid yourself, Bev. Father has never said anything about replacing Mother before. This is it, and I don't think we can stand in his way. Besides," said my serious-minded little brother, "it might be best for all of us. Even though it's been wonderful being here with Aunt Janet, I've really missed Mother so much."

My heart went out to Felix as he sat there on the log playing with a piece of straw that had stuck to his shirt. The poor little fella was only nine, and we'd lost our mom when he was five. Both of us needed a mother. But how could we know what was right?

Felix hastily rubbed away a tear that was threatening to drop. "At least we'll get to see Father next week," he said hopefully.

Just then there was a click of the gate and Uncle Alec came into the barnyard. He stood looking at us with his kind blue eyes that reminded us so much of Father's.

"Well, fellows, I hear we're going to have some company next week. I will be so glad to see my brother and also to meet his friend Elizabeth and her little Caroline." He sat down on the log beside Felix and pulled him over close.

"It's a lot to think about, isn't it, Felix?" he said with understanding. By this time, tears were coming down Felix's chubby little face, and they were stinging my eyelids too. A big change was coming into our lives.

"I—I want Father to be h—happy," sobbed Felix. "But—but how do we know it's the right thing? What if she isn't the right one for Dad? How do you know about th—things like that?" he asked.

"In things like this you just have to trust the grown-ups in your life," Uncle Alec continued. You can trust them to work things out the best for you and your family. Remember? Just like you did when Peter was so sick, and you prayed?

We nodded our heads.

"Well you can pray about this too," he said, giving us some hope to hold onto.

"Why don't we go over to Uncle Roger's and tell him the news? He'll be sure to have something to say about it!" suggested Uncle Alec. "But first you will want to talk about this with your cousins."

Getting up from the log, he gave us both hugs. We loved our uncles—both of them. But somehow Uncle Alec was more understanding the most like Father. Maybe it was because he was a father himself. Uncle Roger was fun to be with though and very special. He was always a big tease. All in all, no boys ever had a better family.

We carried our letter up to the loft, where our little band of cousins had been watching from the loft door window. They had seen our serious talk and tears, and they knew something was up. Not one of them spoke a word until I told them that Father was getting married and bringing his intended bride and her little girl for a visit.

"Is that all?" said Felicity with relief. "I thought maybe your father died or something. I think it's great that you two will have a new mother. Oh, I'd better go see what Mother wants me to do. There will be lots of cooking—maybe even an engagement party while they're here." Felicity was ecstatic that she would have an opportunity to show off her cooking skills and her pretty aprons.

"I say, fellows, that really is good news," said Peter with enthusiasm. "I just never realized how much it means to have two parents until Dad got converted and came back home. It's really wonderful. You'll love having two parents again," he asserted happily.

"Uncle Alec helped a lot," said Felix. "He said to trust the grown-ups and to pray about it, and I'm trying to do that."

"I can't wait to meet your father," said the Story Girl. "I've heard so much about him. And his friend Elizabeth sounds like a nice lady. Let's just hope little Caroline isn't a brat. It sounds like they have plenty of money, and sometimes that isn't good."

"Do you suppose Caroline could be a nasty little kid and push us around and stuff?" said my brother, the worrywart.

"Are you forgetting so quickly, Felix?" I reminded. "We are supposed to trust."

"Yeah. I'm gonna have to work hard at trusting," he said, with a shake of his head.

"I wish *my* father would come home," said the Story Girl, looking off into the distance. "I miss him a lot."

The Story Girl had also lost her mother when she was very young. Felix and I seemed to have a tight bond with her because of that.

"I should get back to work," said Peter. "I just saw your Uncle Roger drive in the lane to the barn. He's back and will be needing me."

We left the loft a lot quieter than we'd come in. There was a lot to think about with the changes that now were coming. Soon we would be going home to another country with a new mother and sister. Later that day, I saw Felix close his eyes and whisper a little prayer. We both had a lot to learn about trust.

A New Mother

"Well, Felicity Feline *is not going to last long today if she doesn't give back my beetle collection and my rocks from the creek bed,*" grumbled Felix. "*Bev, give me some help with her. She's taken all of our nature collections and thrown them outside.*"

Chapter Four

ncle Alec, Aunt Janet, and Uncle Roger got the homesteads ready for our visitors amid much fussing. Felicity was in seventh heaven. She dearly loved to clean and cook and throw orders around. By the day before our guest's arrival, Dan, Felix, and I had just about had it with her. Then she waltzed into our bedroom with mop and broom in hand, making a "clean sweep" of our room by throwing away all of our little treasures and collections that were on the windowsills and dresser.

I was downstairs helping Aunt Janet beat the daylights out of the parlor rug when I heard angry voices upstairs. Running to our bedroom, I found Felicity standing on top of my bed screaming. Felix was holding up a dead mouse.

"Take it, Felicity," he yelled. "Paddy will love it."

"I will not!" she yelled back. "Paddy is not *my* cat and I will *not* take any old dead mouse for him to eat."

The Story Girl, who had run up the steps just behind me, stepped in and grabbed the mouse by the tail. "Oh, for pity sakes, Felicity, don't be such a baby," she stormed. "I never saw such a girl as you."

"Well, *Felicity Feline* is not going to last long today if she doesn't give back my beetle collection and my rocks from the creek bed," grumbled Felix. "Bev, give me some help with her. She's taken all of our nature collections and thrown them outside."

I saw red. "Father won't mind that we have collections and stuff, Felicity. He's used to us and our messy rooms."

"Maybe so, but his intended *fiancée* may not be," responded Felicity. "Mother told me to give this room a good cleaning and air it out. I intend to do just that! You wouldn't believe the mess in that closet. Why, there were shirts I've never seen you wear for months, Bev. They were all wadded up in the back. And the *smell*!" she said, wrinkling her pretty little nose. "I searched and searched until I found that stinky mouse. I asked Felix to take it out for me—but no—he had to dangle it in my face."

She marched over to the window and threw it open. "There! That ought to get the smell out of here! Now I need some help," she demanded. "Would you please take those dirty shirts down to the washing shed? And while you're at it, Bev, bring some clean sheets and blankets from the linen closet."

She was really on her high horse, and I could see there was no hope of any peace until Aunt Janet and the girls had had their fill of cleaning and scrubbing. It wasn't that Aunt Janet's house was dirty. Oh, no! Far from it. It was just that this was a good excuse to really go at it. No healthy germ would *dare* to live there now.

As I gathered up the laundry and started downstairs with it, I thought about our new mother. What would she be like? Would she ruin all the nice times we had with Father? I had heard some terrible stories about stepmothers. It truly was a worry to me, and I knew Felix was scared we wouldn't get along with her. And what about her little daughter? Would she be a pest?

I knew we needed a mother to advise and love us, though. Felix was young—he especially needed a woman's guidance.

"Bev, are you excited?" Felix asked the next morning as we went downstairs for breakfast. "The butterflies in my stomach feel as big as elephants!"

I admitted that I too was excited and nervous. All the way into Charlottetown, Uncle Alec and Aunt Janet chatted, but somehow we just weren't in a talkative mood. When we arrived at the train station, Felix and I sat quietly on the hard benches with Aunt Janet while Uncle Alec went up to the ticket window. Coming back to us, he said that the train was on time and would arrive in about ten minutes—those minutes felt like an eternity.

Suddenly we heard it! The whistle of the train was still a distance away as we gathered our things. Aunt Janet gave Felix a small bouquet she had been holding for him to give to Caroline. I had a lovely one too for our new mother. The train clattered into the station with a great gust of steam and shuddered to a stop, as we stood straining to see, watching the passengers getting off.

"There's Father!" shouted Felix, catching the first glimpse of him. He was helping a little girl down the steps of the train. She was even smaller than I had imagined. A fashionably dressed lady wearing a lovely turquoise traveling coat and hat stood on the steps behind her. Father swung the little girl up in his arms, and the lady took his arm as they started down the platform toward us.

Felix was jumping up and down waving at Father. Unable to wait for them to come to us, he broke away from Uncle Alec and ran the short way down the platform toward our dad. My eyes blurred with tears as I watched Father put Caroline down and open his arms wide for Felix. It had been a long time for my little brother to be away from his parent. Father was laughing and hugging Felix. As I started toward them, he widened his arms for me. There are some moments you will always remember in life, and this is one of them for me.

Father's Elizabeth stood in the background, holding Caroline's hand. As I came out of Father's embrace, I looked into the kindest eyes I had ever seen. They were brimming with unshed tears, and the warmth of her smile melted my heart. I handed her the bouquet as Father said, "These are my dear boys, Elizabeth." Her arms went around me as she thrust her pretty face into the flowers and inhaled deeply. "These are so lovely, Bev. What beautiful flowers."

She had called me "Bev" without my having to tell her I preferred it. Somehow I knew she would be my dearest friend. Now Elizabeth was hugging Felix. It was as if she had always been ours.

"Oh, Caroline, these flowers are for you," said Felix, handing them to our new little sister. On tiptoe, she stretched to give him a kiss on his cheek. "I've always wanted a brother," she said, almost in a whisper. "Now I'll have two," she added, giving me a twinkle and a smile.

After greetings and hugs, Uncle Alec saw to the luggage, and we were on our way to Carlisle.

As we rode along it was so much fun to point out everything we had come to love. "Look, Father, there's the Lake of Shining Waters and Grandfather MacNeill's house, Park Corner," Felix yelled.

"You'll surely have to go there before you leave," said Aunt Janet to Elizabeth. "The whole family is eager to see you again, Alec, and make your acquaintance, Elizabeth. We have a lot of family here on the Island."

"Lots of in-laws and out-laws," Father laughed. "I can't wait to see all of them. We only have one short week, so we'll have to make hay while the sun shines."

I tried to explain to my new mother about all the places Felix was pointing out. I really liked the way she truly listened to what I had to say. She looked me right in the eye, too. I could see why Father loved her.

"Look over there, Father! That's Green Gables, where our cousin Anne Shirley used to live," Felix explained proudly. "'Course she's married now and lives on the other side of the Island. Her aunt Marilla still lives there though. Anne Shirley is an author and quite famous. She's the one who said, 'It's nice to think that tomorrow is a new day with no mistakes in it yet.'

"She's known for saying lots of other things too, like 'kindred spirits' stuff. I think they're called 'Anne-u-risms,'" my funny little brother concluded.

The whole buggy erupted with laughter. We howled and laughed loud enough for Marilla Cuthbert to hear. She came out on the porch and waved her apron to us. When we finally caught our breath from laughing, Father gently told Felix that an *aneurism* is a medical word that means something bad is happening in one of your blood vessels that could kill you.

Felix's comment was classic. "How's a fella s'posed to know about such things?" he grumbled in disgust.

Our new mother patted him on the knee and said, "That's all right, Felix. I just learned a new word too." Felix looked at her like she was a queen and settled back comfortably with her arm around him.

Little Caroline said, "I think you're very smart, Felix. That was a big word to know."

Felix smiled smugly at me. This marriage stuff was going to be good, and we both knew it.

Before we arrived at the farm, Aunt Janet told Father and Elizabeth that we had invited all of the family to an engagement party. It would be held at the end of the week before they were to leave. Father had already explained to us that they would have to go back to Toronto for a few weeks to get ready for the wedding. He said we could stay with our cousins if we wished and then come to Toronto with them for the wedding. After the wedding, Felix and I would be going to Brazil with them so that we could all live together in our new home.

We were glad we didn't have to leave right away. Everything was working out just right. Felix and I had secretly dreaded leaving the farm. We felt torn between our love for Father and our love for the cousins. Now the promise of a new mother and sister made everything seem better.

As we came close to the King Farm Hill Road, Felix jumped up from his seat in the buggy and said excitedly, "Look, Father! Do you see the tree Grandfather King planted—the one you always told us about?" The beautiful old tree was still dressed in its summery green dress, but the leaves were becoming tinged with color, a preview of what fall would bring.

Aunt Janet, ever watchful for our safety, reached across and pulled Felix back down into the seat. Father's fiancée said, "I've heard that story from your father, Felix. To think that all of these beautiful trees have such a rich King history."

"We'll have to plant a tree and name it for your new wife, Father," I said with excitement.

"And Caroline must have her own tree too," Aunt Janet added. "I have an idea. Since you will be married in Toronto, a lot of our family and friends will not be able to attend the wedding. How would it be to make the tree planting a part of the engagement party next Saturday? That would make them feel like part of the festivities."

"That's a wonderful idea, dear," responded Uncle Alec.

"I am overwhelmed by your welcome already, Janet," said Elizabeth. "I can't imagine anyone having a better family. Caroline and I feel very blessed, don't we, honey?" she asked her little girl.

"I am so happy," said my new little sister with a smile, snuggling up to Father in the front seat.

As we drove up in front of the King farmhouse, all the rest of the family was out in front waiting for us. I can't even describe all that went on then—the hugs and greetings and whispered conversations. All of our cousins showed their concern for us.

As I was trying to wrestle a suitcase up the stairs, Dan and Peter dragged me into the pantry and closed the door. I set the luggage down and smiled at them both.

"I know what you're wondering, guys," I said, not even waiting for their questions. "It's fine! In fact, both of them are wonderful. I can see why Father's in love with them—and I feel as if we are already in love with them as well."

Both of them breathed a big sigh of relief. "That's all that matters," said Dan. "Let's go get that trunk, Peter! Typical of girls, they've brought a ton of luggage."

A Surprise for Sara

"It's lovely to be up this early, isn't it?"
said the Story Girl. "The world seems so
different in the morning when the sun is just
beginning to climb out of bed for the day."

Chapter Five

Everyone came for supper the night Father, Elizabeth, and Caroline arrived. Aunt Janet and Felicity had outdone themselves. They had set up a glorious buffet dinner in the beautiful old parlor. After serving ourselves, we all gathered around the huge table in the dining room. Candlelight glittered on the happy faces as Uncle Alec rose and in a solemn voice thanked God for all of his blessings on our family.

After dinner all of our grown-ups, Felix, the Story Girl, and I, went for a walk together to the Carlisle cemetery. The autumn sunset, combined with the wheat fields in the distance, gave a soft golden glow to the old graveyard. Father knelt on one knee and pulled a couple of weeds that grew between Grandfather and Grandmother King's graves. As he knelt there, Uncle Alec came and put his hand on his brother's shoulder. It had been years since Father had been home and seen the graves. Who could imagine his thoughts and memories after such a long absence?

The Story Girl was carrying flowers to put on her mother's grave also. As she did, my father noticed and got up to stand by her. The Story Girl's mother, our Aunt Felicity, had been Father's favorite sister. He put his arm around Sara Stanley and stood with her for some time. The Story Girl, with tears in her eyes, leaned her head comfortably on his shoulder.

"She was a wonderful sister to me, Sara," said Father quietly. After some silence he asked, "Have you heard from your father lately?"

"I usually hear about once a month," answered Sara. "He's in Paris, you know. He seems to be doing well with his art gallery and teaching."

"Poor Blair," Father responded. "When Felicity died, he just couldn't face life here on the Island or in Montreal without her. It's understandable, though. Felicity was the light of his life. He and I had a long conversation about his leaving the Island. He loves you, Sara. It was hard for him to leave, but he thought it best for you to have a family instead of a bachelor father to look after you."

"I really miss him," said Sara sadly, "even though it's wonderful here on the farms with Uncle Roger, Uncle Alec, and Aunt Janet. The cousins and I have such fun together."

"My boys have loved being here," he said. "I know you've been a big part of their happiness, and I do want you to know how much I appreciate it."

56

The Story Girl was carrying flowers to put on her
her's grave also. As she did, my father noticed
got up to stand by her. The Story Girl's mother,
Aunt Felicity, had been Father's favorite sister.
put his arm around Sara Stanley and stood with
for some time. The Story Girl, with tears in her
leaned her head comfortably on his shoulder.
She was a wonderful sister to me, Sara," said
er quietly. After some silence he asked, "Have
heard from your father lately?"
I usually hear about once a month," answered
"He's in Paris, you know. He seems to be doing
with his art gallery and teaching."
Poor Blair," Father responded. "When Felicity
he just couldn't face life here on the Island or in
eal without her. It's understandable, though.
was the light of his life. He and I had a long
sation about his leaving the Island. He loves
ra. It was hard for him to leave, but he thought
or you to have a family instead of a bachelor
o look after you."
ally miss him," said Sara sadly, "even though
derful here on the farms with Uncle Roger,
ec, and Aunt Janet. The cousins and I have
together."
boys have loved being here," he said. "I
u've been a big part of their happiness, and
t you to know how much I appreciate it."

A Surprise for Sara

*"It's lovely to be up this early, isn't it?"
said the Story Girl. "The world seems so
different in the morning when the sun is just
beginning to climb out of bed for the day."*

Chapter Five

Everyone came for supper th[...] Elizabeth, and Caroline arri[...] and Felicity had outdone thems[...] set up a glorious buffet dinner in t[...] parlor. After serving ourselves, we al[...] the huge table in the dining ro[...] glittered on the happy faces as Unc[...] a solemn voice thanked God for al[...] our family.

After dinner all of our grown-[...] Girl, and I, went for a walk tog[...] cemetery. The autumn sunset, [...] wheat fields in the distance, ga[...] to the old graveyard. Father k[...] pulled a couple of weeds [...] Grandfather and Grandmoth[...] knelt there, Uncle Alec came [...] brother's shoulder. It had bee[...] been home and seen the gra[...] his thoughts and memories a[...]

mo[...]
and[...]
our[...]
He [...]
her [...]
eye[...]

Fat[...]
you[...]

Sara[...]
well[...]
"[...]
died,[...]
Mont[...]
Felicit[...]
conve[...]
you, Sa[...]
it best [...]
father [...]
"I [...]
it's wo[...]
Uncle A[...]
such fu[...]
"My[...]
know yo[...]
I do wa[...]

I don't want you readers to think it was a mournful time at the cemetery. It wasn't. It was a sweet and precious time to remember our loved ones who had gone on before. Father stood there in that sacred place, with his arm still around the Story Girl. Little Caroline held her mother's hand and Father's. His peaceful face reflected the closeness and security we had in each other.

I walked back home with the Story Girl, just a bit behind the others. She was very quiet. "A penny for your thoughts," I said.

She smiled and said, "I was just thinking about what your father said. He seems to have a different opinion than our other grown-ups do about my father. You know, Bev, I am hurt by their attitude toward my dad. They sometimes act as if he's a black sheep in the family. I know Aunt Janet thinks he's not very responsible because he doesn't send for me. And she thinks that actresses and artists are all trash. She doesn't give him much credit. You know, he is an artist for royalty all over the world."

"I've heard only good about him from Father," I said. "I wonder why the others here on the island think differently?"

"I don't know," she said with a sigh. "I guess they don't think he loves me or something. I *know* he does. But sometimes I wish . . ."

Her voice trailed off as we caught up with the others near the house. She smiled wistfully, as if she wanted to say more. "Later," I said to her, opening the gate. We always had a good understanding between us. She nodded as we went inside.

The sun had dropped out of sight while we were gone. One golden evening had passed with all of us together. Father and Elizabeth would meet the Carlisle community at church the next morning. For Father it would be a special time for greeting old friends and formally introducing Elizabeth and Caroline.

Saturday was always a time of preparation for Sunday. Everything possible was done ahead of time in order to make Sunday more restful. Soon after our return, Uncle Roger and Father left for Uncle Roger's farm next door, where Father would be staying. As we started upstairs to get ready for bed, Felix asked me a question.

"What were you and the Story Girl talking about on the walk home?"

I dropped a boot on the floor and pulled off a sock before I answered. I didn't really want to bring Felix into it, seeing that it seemed a very private thing for the Story Girl. But Felix was concerned and needed an answer.

"We were wondering why our grown-ups here on the Island have such a different opinion of Blair Stanley than Father does," I answered.

Felix looked at me thoughtfully. "Do you suppose it's because he lost a lot of money before he moved to Paris?" he asked.

I know I looked surprised, because I didn't know what he was talking about. "What do you mean, Felix? I never heard anything about that," I said.

"Sure you did," he said matter-of-factly, as he put on his pajamas. "You remember! Mrs. McClaren, our housekeeper, said it when we were on the train coming here to the Island."

Thinking back, I did remember that, as she traveled with us to the Island, she and Felix were in a big conversation about all of our relatives. I had been reading a book and wasn't paying much attention.

"What did she say?" I asked with interest. I was all ears now.

"Oh, she said Uncle Blair Stanley lost some of the family money. I guess it was really money that belonged to him and Aunt Felicity. You know, the stock market stuff. He didn't mean to do anything wrong, but I guess maybe it looked that way. At least the family thought he wasn't as responsible as he should have been. And then Aunt Felicity got sick and died. It was just too much for him, I guess."

I looked at my brother sadly. "So that's why he went to Paris," I said. "No wonder he hasn't come back. And our poor Story Girl needs her father."

As I crawled into bed, I heard Felix's whispered prayer for the Story Girl and his thanks for our new mother and sister. Things sure seem mixed up sometimes. One minute you're happy, and the next, you're down in the dumps. I guess that's life.

The next day was a happy blur as the whole family went to church and filled the King pews. We ended it that evening in the old King orchard with family vespers. We sat in front of the Pulpit Stone singing hymns as the dusk crept around us—and the silent angels watched over us.

"Isn't this just the way it used to be, Alec?" asked Father.

"Yes, only about now Edward would be ready to preach to us," laughed Uncle Roger. "I can just see him, can't you?"

Everyone laughed at the memory of Uncle Edward, when he was eight years old, preaching with all his "thumps" written into his notes, just like I had done.

For old time's sake, Uncle Alec quoted Psalm 96. The dew was falling as we walked to our homes in thoughtful meditation.

Sing to the LORD a new song;
sing to the LORD, all the earth.
Sing to the LORD, praise his name;

proclaim his salvation day after day.
Declare his glory among the nations,
his marvelous deeds among all peoples.

For great is the LORD and most worthy of praise;
he is to be feared above all gods.
For all the gods of the nations are idols,
but the LORD made the heavens.
Splendor and majesty are before him;
strength and glory are in his sanctuary.

Ascribe to the LORD, O families of nations,
ascribe to the LORD glory and strength.
Ascribe to the LORD the glory due his name;
bring an offering and come into his courts.
Worship the LORD in the splendor of his holiness;
tremble before him, all the earth.

Say among the nations, "The LORD reigns."
The world is firmly established, it cannot be moved;
he will judge the peoples with equity.
Let the heavens rejoice, let the earth be glad;
let the sea resound, and all that is in it;
let the fields be jubilant, and everything in them.
Then all the trees of the forest will sing for joy;
they will sing before the LORD, for he comes,
he comes to judge the earth.

He will judge the world in righteousness
and the peoples in his truth.

On Monday morning, I woke early. Hearing sounds in the kitchen, I dressed and slipped out of the room leaving Felix still asleep. When I got downstairs, Uncle Roger and Father were already there.

"You're up early, Father," I observed. "I thought you might sleep in with all the traveling you've done."

"Not on this Island," said Father. "This is the greatest place on earth early in the morning. Roger and I have been out walking around the farms. The view from the loft of the barn is still as magnificent as I remember it." He stood in the kitchen doorway, looking out and breathing deeply of the pine wood smell that surrounded the old homestead.

Just then Sara Stanley appeared, fresh-eyed and dewy from a good sleep. "Good morning," she said cheerily. "You can tell fall is on the way," she observed, backing up to the wood stove to warm herself. "There's a definite nip in the air."

"Yes," agreed Father. "Don't you just love it, Sara?"

"Indeed I do," she responded. "It's almost my favorite time of year."

"I love summer the most," I said. "Fall and winter always seem so long. One time I dreamed that there were only two seasons in each year—just fall and winter. I kept waiting for spring to come, but it never did."

"That would be like a year without life," said Sara. "I always think that things are dying in the fall and in winter they are dead until spring wakes up the world. Summer is the prime of life.

"I had such a funny dream last night," she said, continuing. "I dreamed that I heard a voice calling me from way down in Uncle Stephen's Walk. 'Sara, Sara, Sara,' it kept calling. I didn't know whose voice it was, and yet it seemed like a voice I knew. I woke up while it was calling. It seemed so real that I could hardly believe it was a dream."

I wondered, when I heard her dream, what could be behind it. After a huge breakfast, Uncle Alec drove Father, Elizabeth, and Caroline over to Park Corner to visit the MacNeills. It was Monday, and wash day, so Aunt Janet stayed home. She had a lot to do with a busy week of company meals to prepare and the upcoming engagement party for Father and Elizabeth. Since the Story Girl didn't seem to be needed just then, I suggested we take a walk down to the far end of the orchard. I had left a book down there which I had been reading on Sunday.

It was still early morning as we passed down Uncle Stephen's Walk through the orchard trees that were just beginning to turn into glorious fall colors.

Paddy trotted along in front of us, waving his plume of a tail proudly.

"It's lovely to be up this early, isn't it?" said the Story Girl. "The world seems so different in the morning when the sun is just beginning to climb out of bed for the day. It's a lovely day for Jasper and Alice Dale to return from their honeymoon. I think they are supposed to be home tonight. We must walk over and welcome them back. Alice would be so pleased and so will Jasper." We took a few more steps and then stood stock-still—staring.

"Why, Bev—who is that in our hammock?" she asked.

I looked. The hammock was hung between the two end trees of Uncle Stephen's Walk, and a man was lying in the hammock, peacefully sleeping with his head pillowed on his overcoat. He seemed to be sleeping easily, lightly, as if he had every right to be there. A suitcase was leaning against a nearby tree.

The man in the hammock had a pointed beard and thick, wavy brown hair. His cheeks were a dusky red and the lashes of his closed eyes were long and silky. He wore a fashionable light gray suit. The sparkle of a diamond ring graced his slender white hand, which hung down over the hammock's edge.

I felt like I knew his face, although I was sure I hadn't seen him before. Had someone described that face to me?

Just then the Story Girl gave a choked little cry. The next moment she had sprung toward the hammock, dropped to her knees, and flung her arms around the man's neck.

"Father! Father!" she cried.

A King Reunion

The happiness went out of me like a
snuffed candle. I hadn't thought about
what life would be like on the hill farm
without the Story Girl. It didn't dawn
on me that I wouldn't be there to know.

Chapter Six

he sleeper in the hammock stirred and opened two large, brilliant hazel eyes. I had seen those eyes before—or ones just like them. They were the Story Girl's eyes staring out from another face. For a moment he gazed blankly at the young lady with brown curls who was embracing him. Then a delighted smile broke over his face, he sprang up, and he hugged her to his heart.

"Sara—Sara—my little Sara! To think I didn't even know you at first glance! But you are almost a woman. And when I saw you last, you were just a little girl of eight. My own little Sara!"

"Oh, Father—sometimes I've wondered if you would ever come back to me," the Story Girl sobbed. I turned and hurried up the Walk, realizing that I was not wanted there just then and wouldn't be missed. Various emotions passed through me, but I was excited to be the one to break the news to our family.

"Aunt Janet," I announced breathlessly as I flew through the kitchen door. "Aunt Janet, Uncle Blair is here."

Aunt Janet, who was kneading bread, turned and lifted her floury hands in surprise. Felicity and Cecily, just coming down for breakfast, stopped still and stared at me.

"Uncle who?" exclaimed Aunt Janet.

"Uncle Blair—the Story Girl's father. You know. He's here."

"Where?" said Aunt Janet, sinking helplessly into a kitchen chair.

"He's down in the orchard. He was asleep in the hammock. We found him there this morning." I felt like I was explaining this to a little child who wasn't able to understand what I was saying.

"Now if that isn't just like Blair," said Aunt Janet, able to speak at last. "Of course, he couldn't come like anyone else. As if we don't have enough company this week," she complained. Then, in a low voice only I heard, she added, "I wonder if he's come to take Sara away?"

The happiness went out of me like a snuffed candle. I hadn't thought about what life would be like on the hill farm without the Story Girl. It didn't dawn on me that I wouldn't be there to know.

Uncle Blair and the Story Girl were just coming out of the orchard. Uncle Blair had his arm around his daughter's waist, and they were laughing and crying at the same time. I had rarely seen the Story

Girl crying like this. But these were happy tears standing in her eyes. I had always known how much she loved her father, though she rarely talked about him. I think that was because she thought her aunts and uncles disapproved of him.

Aunt Janet's welcome was warm enough, though she was thoroughly surprised. Whatever the family thought of Blair Stanley while he was in Paris, they couldn't help but like him when he was there in the flesh. He "had a way about him," as Aunt Janet said. It made him irresistible and lovable. He came in the kitchen door, caught Aunt Janet in his arms, swung her around as though she were a slim schoolgirl, and sat her down with a kiss on her rosy cheeks.

"Sister o' mine, are you never going to grow old?" he said. "Here you are at forty-five with roses of youth in your cheeks. And not a gray hair to show for it either."

"Blair Stanley, you're the one who is always young," laughed Aunt Janet. I could tell she was well pleased with his compliments. "Where in the world did you come from? And what is this I hear about your sleeping all night in the hammock?"

"One day, I just realized how homesick I was to see my little girl and decided to come for a visit," he said. "I was able to schedule a berth on a steamer right away. Everything fell into place, and I arrived in Charlottetown early yesterday. When the train got into Carlisle last night, the stationmaster's son agreed to drive me down to the farm. Nice boy, don't you think? I got here around eleven. The old house was in darkness, and I thought it would be a shame to get all of you out of bed after a hard day's work. The orchard was bathed in moonlight, and my overcoat made a fine pillow. I slept like a baby. And here I am."

"It was very foolish of you," scolded practical Aunt Janet. "These September nights are quite chilly. You might have caught your death of cold—or gotten a bad case of rheumatism."

"So I might. No doubt it was foolish of me," agreed Uncle Blair happily. "It must have been the moonlight. Moonlight, Sister Janet, does strange things to mortal beings. However, I haven't caught cold or rheumatism like a sensible person would. I think the Lord must watch over foolish folk in special ways. I enjoyed my night in the orchard, listening to the murmurs of the wind that stirred sweet, old memories of my youth.

"I had a beautiful dream, Janet," he continued. "I dreamed that the old orchard blossomed again, as it did that spring eighteen years ago. I dreamed that its sunshine was the sunshine of spring, not autumn. There was newness of life in my dream, Janet, and the sweetness of forgotten words."

The Story Girl and I looked at each other, remembering her dream. "Isn't it strange, Bev?" whispered Sara to me. I gulped and nodded. It was strange indeed.

"Well, you'd better come in and have some breakfast," said Aunt Janet. "Do you remember my little girls—Felicity and Cecily?"

"Of course I do," exclaimed Uncle Blair, giving them each a hug. "They haven't changed quite so much as my own baby girl. Why, Sara's a woman, Janet. She's a young woman." He shook his head in wonder.

"She's child enough still," said Aunt Janet quickly.

The Story Girl shook her long brown curls. "I'm fifteen," she said. "And you ought to see me in my long dress, Father."

"No royal commissions will ever tear us apart again, my sweet Sara," Uncle Blair whispered to her. "We will be together forever, until some gallant young man takes you from me. How I could have left you this long is more than I can understand."

I hoped he meant he would stay in Canada, rather than taking Sara away. Then with a stab of pain, I realized Felix and I would be gone as well. How could I want to go and yet want so badly for things to continue as they were? I realized Sara must feel the same way.

Apart from thinking about all the coming changes, we had a happy day with Uncle Blair. He was truly wonderful. When informed that Father was here with his bride-to-be and her young daughter, Uncle Blair was pleased.

"Now I understand why I needed to come at this particular time. How wonderful to see Alan and meet his new family."

I had never seen Sara so happy as she was in her father's presence. Aunt Janet saw it and wept privately. She and Uncle Alec loved Sara like a daughter and would find it difficult to give her up.

Later that day, Sara told us she would be going away with her father in a month. "We will spend the winter in Paris, and I am to go to school there."

We were sitting in the orchard. Our spirits were low, thinking that leaving each other was almost more than we could bear. I truly felt sorry for our cousins who would be left behind. Big tears were rolling down Felicity's face.

"Are you crying because I'm going away, Felicity?" asked the Story Girl.

"Of course I am," she sobbed. "Do you think I've no f—feeling?"

"I didn't think you liked me very much," said Sara honestly.

"I don't wear my heart on m—my sleeve," said poor Felicity. "I wish you could stay."

"I'll have to go sometime," said Sara with sympathy. "It might as well be now, but I will miss all of you so much."

Dinner that evening was again a grand affair. While the women and girls helped Aunt Janet put food on the table, the men spent time talking in the parlor. I overheard the uncles asking Uncle Blair about his art business. They seemed impressed that he had painted portraits for several royal families in different countries. We heard laughter again and again as they talked over old times. *This is good,* I thought.

After dinner the young people went to Golden Milestone to greet the Awkward Man and his bride, who were expected home at sunset. We intended to scatter flowers on the path leading to their front door. It was the Story Girl's idea to do this. She also wanted Uncle Blair to come along. We agreed that it would be best if he would stand out of sight when the newlyweds came home.

"You see, Father, the Awkward Man won't mind us. After all, we're only children and he knows us well," explained the Story Girl. "But if he sees you, it might spoil their homecoming and that would be a shame."

Uncle Blair agreed and hung back, watching from behind some trees. We had collected all the flowers we could gather from both the King farms. It was another clear golden-tinted September evening. As we waited, a great round red moon was rising over Markdale Harbor and peeking down at us. Occasionally the Story Girl would wave to Uncle Blair, who stayed safely out of sight.

"Do you really feel well acquainted with your father?" whispered Sara Ray. "It's been a long time since you've seen him."

"It wouldn't make any difference if a hundred years had passed," laughed Sara Stanley. "I guess we're just 'kindred spirits.'"

"Sh-h-h-h! They're coming," whispered Felicity excitedly.

And then there they were—beautiful Alice, blushing and lovely in the prettiest-of-pretty blue dresses, and Jasper Dale, so happy he had clearly forgotten to be awkward. Their days in Scotland had done them wonders. He lifted her out of the buggy gallantly and led her forward to us, smiling. We ran ahead of them as they came up the walk, scattering our flowers lavishly on the path. Alice Dale walked to the doorstep of her new home over a carpet of blossoms. On the step, they paused and turned toward us as we congratulated them shyly and welcomed them home.

"It was so sweet for you to do this," said the smiling bride.

"It was our pleasure, and we hope you will be happy all the days of your life," said Sara Stanley.

"I'm sure I will," Alice said, turning to her husband. He looked down into her eyes, and we were instantly forgotten. We saw it and slipped away, while Jasper Dale drew his wife into their home and shut the world out.

We scampered away joyously through the moonlit dusk. Uncle Blair joined us at the gate, and the Story Girl asked him what he thought of the bride. Uncle Blair brought out a sketchpad that none of us knew he had with him. There in the gathering dusk, he showed us a drawing of Golden Milestone and Alice and Jasper as they paused in their doorway. We gasped as we saw what he had sketched. The couple, drawn in vivid detail, looked as if they could speak to us. He had done it quickly, as he hid behind the trees. He told us that the sketch would become a large wedding portrait for them. Uncle Blair was truly a genius with art. We could see where the Story Girl got her genius and "way with words."

And so that beautiful day went away from us, quickly slipping through our fingers even as we tried to hold it. Although the day was shadowed by the thoughts of our coming separation, it was another gift from paradise on the Golden Road. From the first blush of dawn to the fall of night, it had given us smiles and tears and left us with exquisite memories.

Bittersweet Times

I'm sorry to say that October was marred by one day of black tragedy—the day Paddy died. After seven years of living a happy cat life, our precious Pat died of poison.

Chapter Seven

That week on the farm with our family passed in a sweet blur. The engagement party served as a fitting finale. Father, Elizabeth, and Caroline left for Toronto amid happy good-byes, because we knew we would see them soon at the wedding. Frankly, Felix and I were glad we weren't required to go with them just yet. It would have been a boring time of wedding stuff, rather than another month to enjoy our cousins.

Life was so full of bittersweet times with our dear friends. We were often heard to say, "This will be the last time we …" or "I wonder if we'll ever …?" The Story Girl and Uncle Blair made our times especially happy. And yet, there were times of sadness, such as the night we talked about the Story Girl leaving her precious Paddy cat behind.

"I know you'll take care of him, but oh, I can hardly bear to leave him behind," Sara said to us. Tears stood in her eyes at the thought of it. "I want you to promise to be kind to him for my sake." We all solemnly assured her that we would.

"I'll g–give him cream every morning and night," said Felicity, who was at the point of tears. "But I'll never be able to look at him without crying. He'll make me think of you."

"Well, I'm not going right away, and neither are Bev and Felix," said the Story Girl, more cheerfully. "Not until the last of October. Let's all agree to make it the most splendid month of all. We won't think about our going at all until we have to, and we won't have any quarrels among us either. We should all forget what's coming and just have all the fun we can."

Felicity sighed and said, "It isn't easy for me to forget things, but I'll try. If you want any more cooking lessons before you go, I'll be glad to teach you."

But the Story Girl shook her head. "No, I don't want to bother about cooking—it just upsets me. I want to enjoy our last month," she insisted.

"Do you remember the time you made the pudding—," began Peter, and suddenly stopped.

"Out of the sawdust?" finished the Story Girl cheerfully. "Don't worry about mentioning it. I don't mind anymore. I can see the fun of it now. Hey, remember when I baked the bread before it was raised enough?"

"People have made worse mistakes than that," said Felicity kindly.

"Such as using tooth-powder—" But here Dan stopped abruptly, remembering that the Story Girl didn't want any quarreling. Felicity turned red but said nothing.

"Just think how much fun we've had together, and how much we've laughed. I hope we will still have fun here on the farm when you've all gone," said Cecily wistfully.

That evening the Story Girl and I drove the cows to pasture after milking. When we came home, we found Uncle Blair in the orchard. He was walking up and down Uncle Stephen's Walk, his hands clasped behind his back and his handsome face lifted up to the sky. When we asked him what he was doing, he said he was thinking of his wife, Aunt Felicity.

"It's almost as if she and I still walk hand in hand here," he said. "She was so young—only eighteen when I met her. There will never be another woman for me. She was my only love—and always will be."

"I wish I could remember her," the Story Girl said with a sigh. "I don't even have a picture of her. Why didn't you paint her, Father?"

"She didn't want me to," he answered. "She had some funny superstition about it. But I intend to do that someday, perhaps when we return to Paris. I am being stirred by all the memories around me. How I loved her! And how happy we were!

"But if you accept human love, you must also accept the pain that lingers when love is gone. Still she is not lost to me and never will be. Nothing is ever really lost to us as long as we remember it. And some sweet day we will be together again, darling Sara. We will see her again," he said with certainty. Uncle Blair looked up at the evening star, and we saw he had forgotten we were there. We slipped away, leaving him alone in the memory-haunted orchard.

The Story Girl had asked us to try to make our last month together beautiful, and nature seemed to want to help in that regard. Nothing could have been more beautiful than the maple trees that year. All the glow and radiance and joy of the earth's heart seemed to have broken loose to express it. It was again time for apple picking, and we worked joyously with Uncle Blair and the Story Girl.

One Saturday afternoon, when the others were busy with chores, the Story Girl and I went for a walk with Uncle Blair. Sara and I, as the oldest cousins, loved to do things together. It seemed we had dreams and aspirations the others did not yet have. At times we seemed like children and enjoyed childish things, but there was no doubt that things were changing about the way we looked at life. It was at those times we enjoyed adult companions like Uncle Blair.

"Where are we going?" the Story Girl asked her father.

"I want one more ramble in the Prince Edward Island woods before I leave Canada, and I would enjoy it more with you two young people," he replied.

"I always feel so *satisfied* in the woods," said Sara, as we began our walk. "Trees seem like such friendly things."

"They are the most friendly things in God's creation," said Uncle Blair. "To hold conversation with the pines, whisper secrets to the poplars, and listen to the tales of old romance the beech trees tell, is to learn about real companionship."

"It's so easy to *believe* things in the woods," observed the Story Girl.

"I have to sketch this," said Uncle Blair, getting out his sketchpad and making some quick strokes that would remind him of this spot forever.

We found a little brook where we refreshed ourselves with pure, sparkling water. I have never forgotten that afternoon, or that place touched with the magic of autumn, the sounds of the forest, and the canopy of silence.

I'm sorry to say that October was marred by one day of black tragedy—the day Paddy died. After seven years of living a happy cat life, our precious Pat died of poison. We didn't know where he picked it up, but we found him on the doorstep at dawn one frosty morning so near death that we knew there was no hope. The Story Girl held him close, stroking his glossy fur, letting her tears drop on his limp body. He gave one pitiful little mew—a long quiver—and he was gone.

"It doesn't seem as if it can be true," sobbed Cecily.

"If a cat has nine lives like they say, he's had many," cried Felicity. "This time yesterday he was full of life and drank two dishes of cream."

"It may be for the best after all," said the Story Girl tearfully. "I've been feeling so bad about leaving him. I know he would have missed me and might never have been really contented again."

"I wish we could believe that cats go to heaven," said Cecily. "Do you think that's possible, Uncle Blair?"

"I'm afraid not," he said. Putting his arm around Sara, he tried to console her in her sadness. "I wish we could believe that, but heaven is just for people."

Aunt Janet in her practical way said, "Well, get him buried, and let's get on with the apple picking."

There was no way we could bury our furry friend in such an off-handed way. We decided his funeral would be at sunset that night in the orchard he loved. Sara Ray sobbed as the boys dug his grave.

"We never know what a day will bring forth. That's in the Bible," she added. We laid him to rest, having decided not to sing a hymn or read a Scripture verse. He was, after all, only a cat, and the Story Girl had the say about his funeral.

"We don't want to make it ridiculous," she said. "But we will have a real obituary about him in *Our Magazine* this month."

"Peter is going to cut his name on a stone, but we mustn't let the grown-ups know. They may not think it's right," said Felicity.

After many tears and a kind word of comfort from Uncle Blair, we left the orchard. But not even Uncle Blair could make us feel better when Paddy wasn't there at milking time the next· evening. Felicity cried the whole time she was straining the milk. Many human beings have gone to their graves without the mourning and sadness with which our gray pussycat went to his.

The end of October was coming fast, and we knew that the final issue of *Our Magazine* needed to be written. No one wanted to do it because it seemed like such a final closing to our time together. But I begged the others to contribute their columns and they did so. Most of the articles were less than outstanding so I won't quote them, but I did think the obituary written about Paddy was good. Felix wrote the text and Sara Ray added the poetry at the end.

Obituary

On October 18, Patrick Grayfur, Esq., departed for the place where good cats go when they die. He was only a feline, but he had been our faithful friend for a long time, and we aren't ashamed to feel sorry for him. There are lots of people who are not as friendly and as much of a gentleman as Paddy was, and he was a great mouser. We buried poor Pat in the orchard he loved, and we will never forget him. We have resolved that whenever the date of his death comes around, we'll bow our heads and pronounce his name at the hour of his funeral. If we are anyplace where we can't say the name out loud, we'll whisper it.

"Farewell, dearest Paddy, in all the years that are to be,
We'll cherish your memory faithfully."

The night the newspaper came out, we sat around and read it to each other. "I know we can't carry it on after you leave, Bev," the Story Girl said, "but it's really been fun. I think you will be a real newspaper editor some day," she declared.

"How do you know he will?" asked Felicity.

"I can't tell futures," she answered. "But I bet I can make some good guesses." She turned to me. "I imagine you will write books too, and travel all over the world."

She looked at Felix. "My guess is that Felix will always be chubby, and he will be a grandfather with a long black beard before he's fifty."

"I won't!" cried Felix. "I hate whiskers. Maybe I can't help being a grandfather but I *can* help having a beard."

Ignoring him, she went on. "I think Peter will probably become a minister, and Dan a farmer, who will marry and have at least eleven children."

Despite the protests, she continued. "I picture Felicity as a minister's wife. She will be a perfect housekeeper, of course, and teach a Sunday school class. I imagine her being very happy all the days of her life."

"What about her husband? Will he be happy?" asked Dan, teasing.

"I guess he'll be as happy as *your* wife," retorted Felicity with a red face.

"He'll be the happiest man in the world," declared Peter warmly.

"And I imagine that Sara Ray will live to be a hundred and go to dozens of funerals," she said, recalling a funny comment Sara once made. "I bet you will finally learn not to cry once you are seventy!"

"What about me?" asked Cecily. "What do you imagine will become of me?"

But suddenly the Story Girl stopped speaking and her eyes looked sad.

The Curve in the Road

In later years, I wondered about that
night. Perhaps the Story Girl realized what
we all had secretly thought—our sweet
Cecily was not strong. She would probably
not live to be a grandmother, full of long life,
as Felix, and indeed all of us, would.

Chapter Eight

hat about me?" said Cecily disappointedly. The Story Girl looked very tenderly at Cecily—at the smooth little brown head and the soft, shining eyes. She looked at the cheeks that were often over-rosy after slight exercise and at the little sunburned hands that were always busy doing faithful work or a quiet kindness. Her eyes grew sad and far-reaching, as if looking into the mists of hidden years.

"I can't imagine anything half good enough for you, dearest," she said, slipping her arm around Cecily. "You deserve everything that is good and lovely. But you know I've only been guessing at things for the fun of it. Only God knows what is going to happen to any of us. We can't know his plans."

"Perhaps you know more than you think," said Sara Ray. She was hoping Sara Stanley was right— at least about the being married part.

"Don't be ridiculous, Sara Ray," said the Story Girl. "It was just in fun."

"But can't you say anything about me?" persisted Cecily.

"Everybody you meet will love you as long as you live," said the Story Girl. "There! That's the very nicest thing I can tell you. Now we must go in before you start coughing again."

We went inside though Cecily was still a little disappointed. In later years, I wondered about that night. Perhaps the Story Girl realized what we all had secretly thought—our sweet Cecily was not strong. She would probably not live to be a grandmother, full of long life, as Felix, and indeed all of us, would. Before the bloom of youth faded, she would be in heaven with the one she loved. Cecily's feet were never to leave the Golden Road. She would go before us to a place prepared for her.

It was the evening before the Story Girl and Uncle Blair were ready to leave. We had one more time together in the orchard where we had spent so many happy hours. We had taken a walk and visited all of the places that were dear to us. The Spruce Wood, the fields and hills, the dairy, Grandfather's willow tree, Paddy's grave, Uncle Stephen's Walk, and now the Pulpit Stone. We sat down in the grass that was turning October nut brown and feasted on little jam turnovers Felicity had made especially for the occasion.

"I wonder if we'll ever all be together again," sighed Cecily.

"I wonder if we'll ever get jam turnovers like this again," said the Story Girl, trying to be light without making much of a success of it.

"If Paris weren't so far away I could send you a box of goodies now and then," said Felicity sadly. "Who knows what they'll give you to eat over there."

"Oh, the French have the reputation of being the best cooks in the world," said the Story Girl. "But I know they can't beat your jam turnovers and plum puffs, Felicity. I'll be craving them, I know."

"If we ever do meet again, we'll all be grown up," said Felicity gloomily. "We'll be different, and everything will be changed."

"That isn't all bad, you know," said Cecily. "Just think—last New Year's Eve we were wondering what would happen this year, and a lot has happened that we never expected."

"If things never happened, life would be pretty dull," responded the Story Girl. "We've had so many good times here."

"And some bad times too," reminded Felix. "Remember when Dan ate the bad berries last summer?"

"And the time we were so scared over that bell ringing in the house?" grinned Peter.

"And judgment day?" added Dan.

"And when Peter was dying of the measles?" said Felicity. "That was the worst."

"Do you remember when we bought the picture of God?" asked Peter.

"I wish I could *forget* it," said Sara Ray. "And I can't forget what the bad place is like either, ever since Peter preached that sermon on it."

"When you get to be a real minister, you'll have to preach that sermon over again, Peter," said Dan with a grin. "My Aunt Jane used to say that people need a sermon on the bad place once in a while."

"Do you remember the time I ate cucumbers and drank milk to make me dream?" asked Cecily.

We all laughed and opened our Dream Books. We had brought them along to help us remember. Each of us read one of our favorite dreams, and then we gathered around the old well and had a cup of its water for old times' sake. We started to sing "Auld Lang Syne" and before the first line, "Should old acquaintance be forgot," Sara Ray began to cry. What else was new? She would cry until she was seventy, the Story Girl had said. I was just glad I wouldn't have to hear it much longer.

Then, as we turned to leave the orchard, Sara Stanley said she wanted to ask a favor of us. "Don't say good-bye to me tomorrow morning when we leave."

"Why not?" asked Felicity.

"Because it's such a hopeless sort of word. Let's not say it at all. Just see me off with a wave of your hands. It won't seem half so bad then. And don't any of you cry if you can help it. I want to remember you all smiling."

We went out of the old orchard for the last time, while the autumn-night wind was making its weird music in the leaves. The gate made a loud click as we left our memories behind.

The next morning was rosy, clear, and frosty. Everyone was up early since Uncle Blair and Sara had to leave in time to catch the nine o'clock train. The horse was harnessed and waiting at the door, with Uncle Alec in the driver's seat. Aunt Janet was crying, but none of us were. We were trying very hard to do as Sara had asked. The Awkward Man and Mrs. Dale came to see their favorite on her way. Mrs. Dale had brought Sara a large bunch of beautiful red chrysanthemums, and the Awkward Man gave her another little old book from his library. I could tell the Story Girl was thrilled with the gift. She held the little book to her heart and gave him a kiss on his cheek.

"Read it when you are happy or sad, discouraged or hopeful," he said quite gracefully.

"He has really improved very much since he got married," Felicity whispered to me. "Aren't they a lovely looking couple?"

I had to agree that they made a handsome pair. On the night before, Uncle Blair had given them the wedding portrait he had painted. It was framed beautifully and greatly admired by us all. It was such a thoughtful gift, as the camera had just been invented and wedding portraits were not yet plentiful.

Sara Stanley wore a new smart traveling suit and a little blue hat with a white feather. She looked terribly grown-up and lost to us already.

Sara Ray had vowed the night before that she would be up in the morning for the farewell. But Judy Pineau came to say that, with her usual luck, Sara Ray had a sore throat, and her mother wouldn't let her come. So she had written her parting words to the Story Girl in a three-cornered pink note. She had underlined words to emphasize her feelings as she usually did.

My own darling friend:

Words cannot express my feelings over not being able to say good-bye to one I so fondly adore. When I think that I cannot see you again, my heart is almost too full for utterance. But mother says I cannot and I must obey. But I'll be present in spirit. It just breaks my heart that you are going so far away. You have always been so kind to me and never hurt my feelings as others have. I shall miss you so

*much. But I earnestly hope and pray that you
will be happy and prosperous wherever you
are and not be seasick on the great ocean. I
hope you will find time among your many
duties to write me a letter once in a while. I
shall always remember you and hope that you
will remember me. I hope we will meet again
sometime, but if not, may we meet in a far
better world where there are no sad partings.*

> *Your true and loving friend,*
> *Sara Ray*

"Poor little Sara Ray," said the Story Girl after
reading it. She slipped the tear-stained note into her
pocket. "She isn't a bad little soul, and I'm sorry I
can't see her once more. Maybe it's just as well
because she'd be sure to cry."

The Story Girl, true to her word, didn't cry,
though her eyes were unusually bright with unshed
tears. They threatened to spill over when she hugged
Cecily. Did she perhaps know she would not see her
precious friend again on this earth?

When she hugged Felicity, she warned, "Don't you
dare cry, Felicity. Oh, you dear darling people. I love
you so much, and I will go on loving you always."

Aunt Janet was the last to hug her, and our
aunt's tears were very evident. "Oh Blair, watch over
her well," she cried. "Remember, you must now be

father *and* mother to her. You must find a good companion and housekeeper who will help you. Be sure you don't allow her to go anywhere in Paris without a proper chaperone."

The Story Girl ran over to the buggy and climbed in. Uncle Blair followed her after receiving Uncle Roger's handshake and hug. It surely seemed as though there was a new understanding between the uncles and Blair Stanley that pleased everyone.

"Come to see us in Paris, Roger," invited Uncle Blair. "You are footloose and fancy-free with no wife, and we could show you a wonderful time."

"Oh, do come, Uncle Roger," begged the Story Girl. "We would dearly love to see all of you, especially Felicity. You must come and sample French pastry."

Although unknown to us at the time, our family would visit them in Paris. It seemed such a slim possibility then, but times were changing and world travel was not as difficult as it once had been. Who would ever believe that our family would move to South America and our Father would become so prominent?

Felix and I stood with Peter, watching with tears in our eyes. Now that apple-picking season was ended, Peter would go on to the Markdale School. We didn't know at the time what a fine mind Peter had, nor how well he would excel at school and seminary. He would truly have made his Aunt Jane proud.

Felix and I would leave the next day, with the entire family, for Father's wedding in Toronto. Even Uncle Roger would go to the wedding this time, leaving a neighbor to watch over the farm until he returned.

The Story Girl's arms were full of Mrs. Dale's flowers, held up close to her face, and her beautiful eyes shone softly as she looked at us over the top of them. No good-byes were said, but she blew special kisses to us. We all smiled bravely and waved our hands as they drove out the lane and onto the moist, red road lined with shadows from the fir trees.

We stayed in our places, for we knew we would see them again when they came to the open curve in the road. Sara had promised to wave a last farewell as they passed around it. We watched the curve in silence, standing in a sorrowful little group in the sunshine of that autumn morning. The delight of the world had been ours on the Golden Road. It had enticed us with daisies and rewarded us with roses. Imagination, careless and sweet, had visited us. Laughter had been our playmate, and fearless hope our guide. But now the shadow of change hung over our Golden Road.

"There she is," cried Felicity.

The Story Girl stood up and waved her chrysanthemums at us. We waved wildly back until the buggy had driven around the curve. Then we went slowly and silently back to the house, the Story Girl was gone, and a new chapter was beginning on the Golden Road.

Lucy Maud Montgomery
1908

Lucy Maud Montgomery
1874-1942

Anne of Green Gables was the very first book that Lucy Maud Montgomery published. In all, she wrote twenty-five books.

Lucy Maud Montgomery was born on Prince Edward Island. Her family called her Maud. Before she was two years old, her mother died and she was sent to live with her mother's parents on their farm on the Island. Her grandparents were elderly and very strict. Maud lived with them for a long time.

When she was seven, her father remarried. He moved far out west to Saskatchewan, Canada, with his new wife. At age seventeen, she went to live with them, but she did not get along with her stepmother. So she returned to her grandparents.

She attended college and studied to become a teacher—just like Anne in the Avonlea series. When her grandfather died, Maud went home to be with her grandmother. Living there in the quiet of Prince Edward Island, she had plenty of time to write. It was during this time that she wrote her first book, *Anne of Green Gables*. When the book was finally accepted, it was published soon after. It was an immediate hit, and Maud began to get thousands of letters asking for more stories about Anne. She wrote *Anne of Avonlea, Chronicles of Avonlea, Anne of the Island, Anne of Windy Poplars, Anne's House of Dreams, Rainbow Valley, Anne of Ingleside,* and *Rilla of Ingleside*. She also wrote *The Story Girl* and *The Golden Road*.

When Maud was thirty-seven years old, Ewan Macdonald, the minister of the local Presbyterian Church in Canvendish, proposed marriage to her. Maud accepted and they were married. Later on they moved to Ontario where two sons, Chester and Stewart, were born to the couple.

Maud never went back to Prince Edward Island to live again. But when she died in 1942, she was buried on the Island, near the house known as Green Gables.

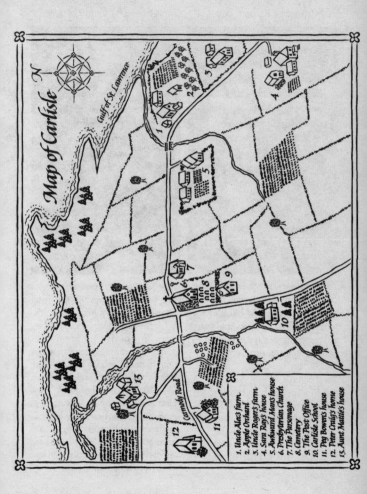

Map of Carlisle

Gulf of St. Lawrence

N

1. Uncle Alec's farm
2. Apple Orchard
3. Uncle Roger's farm
4. Awkward Man's house
5. Sara Ray's house
6. Presbyterian Church
7. The Parsonage
8. Cemetery
9. The Post Office
10. Carlisle School
11. Peg Bowen's house
12. Peter Craig's home
13. Aunt Mattie's house

Carmody Road

The King Cousins

(Book 1)
By L.M. Montgomery
Adapted by Barbara Davoll

Measles, Mischief, and Mishaps

(Book 2)
By L.M. Montgomery
Adapted by Barbara Davoll

Sara Stanley, the Story Girl, can captivate anyone who will listen to her tales. In this first book of the series, brothers Beverley and Felix arrive on Prince Edward Island to spend the summer with their cousins on the King Homestead. These curious and imaginative children set out to find out about the existence of God. What follows are childhood antics, tall-tales, and legends from a time long past.

SOFTCOVER 0-310-70598-3

As Sara Stanley continues to spin her wonderful stories, the King Cousins get into a load of trouble. First, they convince their neighbor, Sara Ray, to disobey her mother and go to a magic lantern show with them. Then Sara Ray gets very sick with measles and the Story Girl thinks it is all her fault. Then Dan loses a baby he is watching. And if that's not enough, he defiantly eats poisonous berries and becomes very ill. Here are more childhood antics, tall-tales, and legends from a time long past.

SOFTCOVER 0-310-70599-1

Available now at your local bookstore!

zonder**kidz**

Summer Shenanigans (Book 3)
By L.M. Montgomery
Adapted by Barbara Davoll

The King cousins read a dreaded prophecy about judgment day. When they hear a mysterious, ghostly ringing bell, they are frightened nearly out of their wits, thinking it has something to do with the end of the world. They become so frightened that the Story Girl refuses to tell any more stories. This book is filled with shenanigans and rollicking summer days as the King cousins try to make the most ot their time together on Prince Edward Island.

SOFTCOVER 0-310-70600-9

Available now at your local bookstore!

Dreams, Schemes, and Mysteries

(Book 4)

By L.M. Montgomery

Adapted by Barbara Davoll

Toward the end of the cousins' summer together on Prince Edward Island, the Story Girl has an idea for them all to do together—a preaching contest followed by a bitter-apple-eating contest. Both contests end in near disaster as Peter, a neighbor boy, falls deathly ill. The kids decide that lots of prayer and good behavior will make him well. And it works. Things quiet down until a letter arrives saying that at long last the mysterious blue chest stored at the King Homestead can be opened and its secret revealed.

SOFTCOVER 0-310-70601-7

Available now at your local bookstore!

zonder**kidz**

Winter on the Island
(Book 5)
By L.M. Montgomery
Adapted by Barbara Davoll

The King cousins and their friends celebrate Christmas as winter overtakes the community on Prince Edward Island, slowing life's pace. With plenty of time on their hands, the Story Girl and Bev start a newspaper, and before long everyone has a story for it. Antics and exploits abound, and when a blizzard catches the children away from home, they have their biggest adventure yet!

Softcover 0-310-70859-1

Wedding Wishes and Woes

(Book 6)
By L.M. Montgomery
Adapted by Barbara Davoll

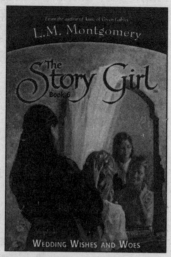

As spring roars in like a lion, the King cousins experience a whirl of adventures—not all of them fun: Dan is knocked unconscious, a boy annoys Cecily, and Sara's cat disappears. But things take a turn for the better when Aunt Olivia announces she's getting married, and Peter's once-alcoholic father proclaims he's become a Christian. Is life always this full of changes?

SOFTCOVER 0-310-70860-5

Available now at your local bookstore!

zonder**kidz**

Midnight Madness and Mayhem
(Book 7)
By L.M. Montgomery
Adapted by Barbara Davoll

Winds of Change
(Book 8)
By L.M. Montgomery
Adapted by Barbara Davoll

The Story Girl has moved in with the King cousins now that Aunt Olivia has married and moved to Nova Scotia. But just when it seems as if things are getting back to normal, a series of adverse events have the children wondering how to get along with their neighbors, while a pair of old romantic mysteries might—or might not—be resolved. Sara knows the secret —but will she tell?

SOFTCOVER 0-310-70861-3

When a letter arrives from South America, Bev and Felix learn their father is coming for them—and he is bringing his new wife-to-be! To add to the excitement, Sara is surprised when her father returns from Paris. Soon this large family will be scattered, so the cousins try to make the most of their remaining time together. What will life on the Island be like without the Story Girl?

SOFTCOVER 0-310-70862-1

zonder**kidz**.

We want to hear from you. Please send your comments
about this book to us in care of zreview@zondervan.com. Thank you.

Grand Rapids, MI 49530
www.zonderkidz.com